LIVING FOSSILS

Horseshoe Crabs

Annie Wendt Hemstock

PowerKiDS press.

New York

Published in 2015 by The Rosen Publishing Group, Inc.
29 East 21st Street, New York, NY 10010

First Edition

Editor: Sarah Machajewski
Book Design: Mickey Harmon

Photo Credits: Cover (horseshoe crabs) Oleg Moiseyenko/Moment Open/Getty Images; cover, pp. 1–3, 4, 6, 8, 10, 12, 14, 16, 18, 19, 20, 22–24 (logo) Bplanet/Shutterstock.com; cover, pp. 1–24 (border texture) Markus Gann/Shutterstock.com; p. 4 (fossil) koi88/Shutterstock.com; p. 5 Wasu Watcharadachaphong/Shutterstock.com; pp. 5, 6, 9, 10, 13, 14, 17, 18, 20 (caption box border) little Whale/Shutterstock.com; pp. 5, 6, 9, 10, 13, 14, 17, 18, 20 (caption box inside) Yuri Samsonov/Shutterstock.com; p. 7 (horseshoe crabs) Jeff Rotman/The Image Bank/Getty Images; p. 7 (sand) Paul Maguire/Shutterstock.com; pp. 8, 11 (horseshoe crab) OlegD/Shutterstock.com; p. 9 Mariusz S. Jurgielewicz/Shutterstock.com; p. 11 (sand) Phatthanit/Shutterstock.com; pp. 12, 13 (eggs) Robert F. Sisson/National Geographic/Getty Images; p. 15 Jana Shea/Shutterstock.com; p. 16 (bi[illegible]) Elliotte Rusty Harold/Shutterstock.com; p. 17 Dawn J Benko/Shutterstock.com; p. 18 (raw crabs) M R/Shutterstock.com; p. 19 Brian D Cruickshank/Lonely Planet Images/Getty Images; p. 21 Raul Touzon/National Geographic/Getty Images; p. 22 The Washington Post/The Washington Post/Getty Images.

Library of Congress Cataloging-in-Publication Data

Hemstock, Annie Wendt.
Horseshoe crabs / Annie Hemstock.
pages cm. — (Living fossils)
Includes index.
ISBN 978-1-4777-5826-7 (pbk.)
ISBN 978-1-4777-5824-3 (6 pack)
ISBN 978-1-4777-5822-9 (library binding)
1. Merostomata—Juvenile literature. I. Title.
QL447.7.H46 2015
595.4'92—dc23

2014022760

Manufactured in the United States of America

CPSIA Compliance Information: Batch #CW15PK: For Further Information contact Rosen Publishing, New York, New York at 1-800-237-9932

Contents

From Ages Past

Have you ever been to the ocean? If you have, you may have seen a kind of animal that's very old. This animal is older than flying insects. It's even older than dinosaurs! This ancient creature is the horseshoe crab.

Horseshoe crabs aren't really crabs. Like crabs, insects, and spiders, they're **arthropods**. They make up a class of arthropods called Merostomata. This means "legs attached to the mouth."

Horseshoe crabs have been on Earth for over 500 million years. They haven't changed much in all that time. That's why they're called "living fossils."

What's hiding under these hard shells?
Read on to find out!

Beaches and Bays

There are four kinds of horseshoe crabs. One kind lives off the eastern coast of North and Central America. The others live off the coasts of Asia and India.

Horseshoe crabs spend most of their life in the water. They only come on land to **mate** and lay eggs. They lay eggs in bays that are safe from waves.

Young horseshoe crabs stay near the bays where they **hatched**. They live on the **tidal flats**. When the tide goes out, they bury themselves in the sand. Adult horseshoe crabs live in deeper water.

This photo shows the four different kinds of horseshoe crabs that live around the world.

Asia
India
Asia
North and Central America

A Hard Exterior

A hard shell covers the horseshoe crab's body. The front part is called the prosoma. Six pairs of legs are attached to it. The middle part is called the opisthosoma. Special **gills**, called book gills, are found here. The horseshoe crab's tail is called the telson. It helps the horseshoe crab flip over when it's on its back.

FOSSIL FACTS

If the horseshoe crab is stuck on its back, it digs its tail into the sand. Planting its tail allows the horseshoe crab to lift its body so it can turn over.

A horseshoe crab has 10 eyes. Two are **compound eyes**. They help the horseshoe crab find a mate. Some eyes can only tell light from dark. The horseshoe crab even has eyes underneath its body. They help it stay right side up!

Eat, Breathe, and Move

Each part of a horseshoe crab's body has a special purpose. Its gills are called book gills because they look like the pages of a book. Book gills take in oxygen from the water. They also help the horseshoe crab swim.

A horseshoe crab has six pairs of legs. The legs surround its mouth. The first pair isn't used for walking. Instead, it's used to bring pieces of food to the horseshoe crab's mouth. **Bristles** that cover the legs help crush the horseshoe crab's food. It eats **mollusks**, worms, and other small **marine** animals. It also eats algae.

The horseshoe crab's hard shell helps protect everything that's hidden underneath it.

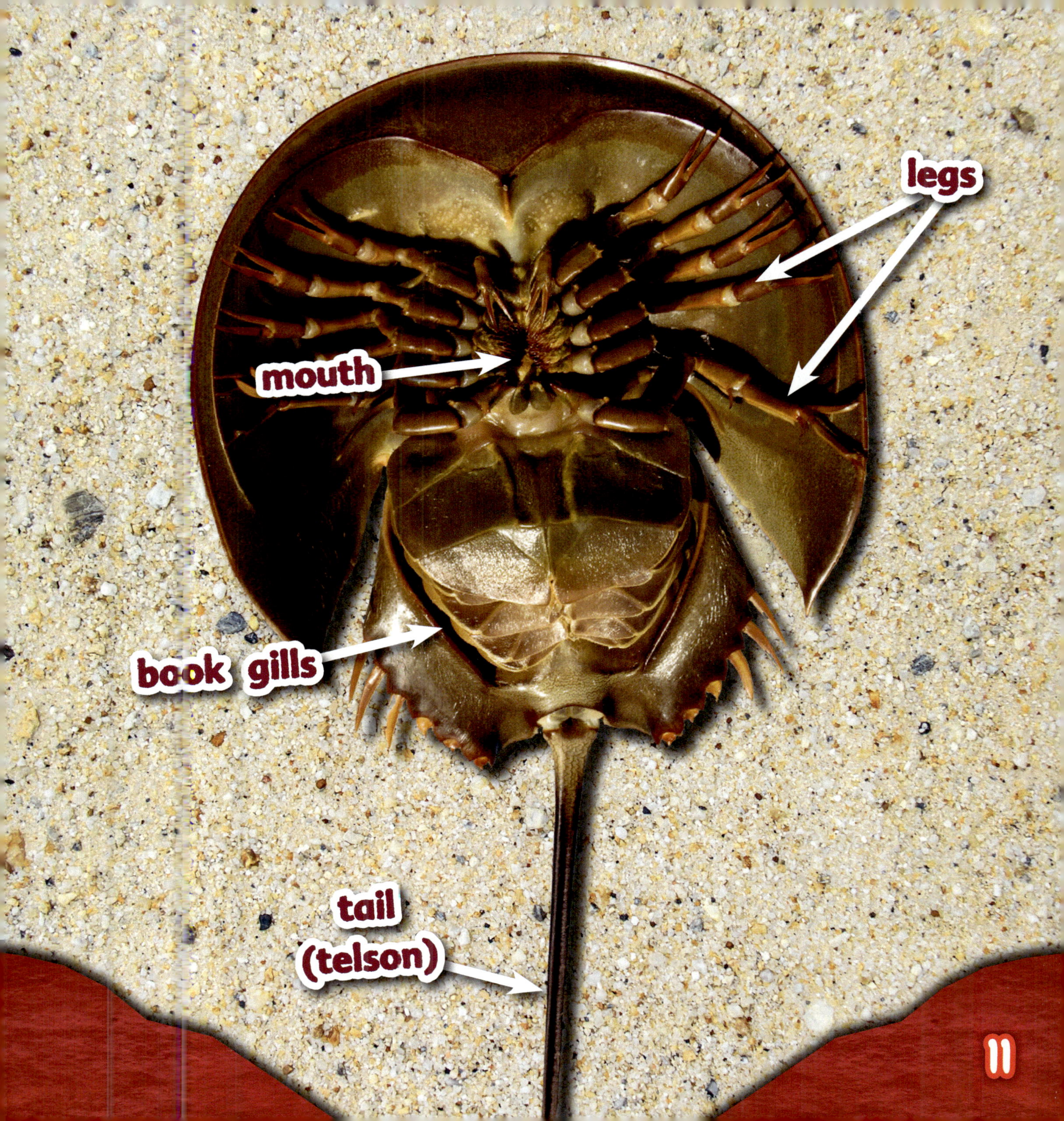
legs
mouth
book gills
tail
(telson)

The Cycle of Life

Horseshoe crab eggs hatch in the sand. Baby horseshoe crabs are called larvae. Larvae are only about 0.4 inch (1 cm) long, but they look like adult horseshoe crabs. The larvae dig out of the sand and move into the water. They already know how to swim!

Horseshoe crabs shed their shell as they get bigger. This is called molting. **Juvenile** horseshoe crabs molt several times a year for the first few years of their life. After that, they only shed their shell once a year. A horseshoe crab is considered an adult when it's old enough to mate.

FOSSIL FACTS

A horseshoe crab replaces its old shell with a new, bigger shell that fits its larger body.

These baby horseshoe crabs look like tiny adults.

Coming Ashore

Juvenile horseshoe crabs spend most of their time in shallow water. They live in areas that aren't affected by waves. They move to deeper water as they grow. Adult horseshoe crabs move to the beaches in late spring. That's their spawning season, which is a time when they find a mate and lay eggs.

Male horseshoe crabs arrive first, but the females dig the nests. Each female lays thousands of eggs in her nest. In all, a female horseshoe crab lays about 90,000 eggs a year. They do this every year for the rest of their lives!

Thousands of horseshoe crabs arrive in Delaware Bay each year for their spawning season.

FOSSIL FACTS

Spawning time usually happens at night, when the tide is high and the moon is bright in the sky!

Eat and Be Eaten

Every living creature is part of an **ecosystem**. Each creature depends on the other creatures in its ecosystem to survive. Horseshoe crabs are an important part of the ecosystem at Delaware Bay. It's one of their biggest spawning areas. Their eggs become food for at least 11 kinds of birds in the Delaware Bay ecosystem.

The red knot is a shorebird that's part of this special ecosystem. Red knots **migrate** many miles to reach their resting places. Delaware Bay is a good place for them to rest and find food. Can you see how red knots and other birds need horseshoe crabs to survive?

red knot

FOSSIL FACTS

Birds aren't the only animals that feast on horseshoe crab eggs. Several kinds of fish, crabs, and sea turtles enjoy them, too!

All kinds of shorebirds depend on horseshoe crabs to survive.

The Helpful Horseshoe Crab

Horseshoe crabs help shorebirds, but they help people, too! People in some parts of the world eat horseshoe crab eggs. Sometimes people use horseshoe crabs as bait to catch other kinds of food. They were even once used as **fertilizer**.

Studying horseshoe crabs teaches us a lot about nature—and ourselves.

We've learned a lot from horseshoe crabs. Their eyes have taught us more about our own eyes. Scientists have used horseshoe crabs to make bandages that help burns heal faster. They've also used the horseshoe crab's special blood to help us see if there are germs in our medicine. The things we've learned from horseshoe crabs have saved many lives.

Helping Our Horseshoe Crabs

Horseshoe crabs have been around for hundreds of millions of years, but there aren't as many as there used to be. One reason is because people use them as bait. Some people have tried to help horseshoe crabs by making bait bags for fishermen. Bait bags make bait last longer so fisherman don't use as many horseshoe crabs.

Horseshoe crabs can be in danger if they're stuck on their backs. If they don't flip over, they could die. If you see a horseshoe crab on its back, turn it right side up! This helps the horseshoe crab survive and get back to the ocean.

It's safe to pick up a horseshoe crab, but be careful—if your fingers get caught near its mouth, it could bite you.

FOSSIL FACTS

You can help rescue a horseshoe crab that's stuck upside down. Gently grab the edge of its shell and turn it back over. Never pick it up by its tail—it could break!

Looking Ahead

Horseshoe crabs have been around for a very long time. Although they've survived for millions of years, it's our job to make sure they survive well into the future.

There's a lot we can do to help horseshoe crabs. Learning about what they need to live, keeping their ecosystems healthy, and not catching too many are all ways to help. These efforts, and more, will make sure this living fossil is around for many years to come.

Glossary

arthropods: Any of a group of animals with jointed legs, hard outer coverings, and no backbone.

bristle: A short, stiff hair on an animal's body.

compound eye: An animal's eye made up of several repeating units that are used to see.

ecosystem: A community of living things and the surroundings in which they live.

fertilizer: Something put in soil to help crops grow.

gill: A body part used by some marine animals to breathe.

hatch: To break out of a shell.

juvenile: Having to do with youth or being young.

marine: Having to do with the ocean.

mate: To come together to make babies. Also, one of two animals that come together to make babies.

migrate: To move from one place to another.

mollusk: An animal without a backbone and with a soft body and, often, a shell.

tidal flat: A coastal wetland that forms in bays from the water and mud deposited by a body of water.

Index

Websites

Due to the changing nature of Internet links, PowerKids Press has developed an online list of websites related to the subject of this book. This site is updated regularly. Please use this link to access the list: www.powerkidslinks.com/fos/crab